Sister Beatrice

Sister Beatrice

Translated into English Verse from the Manuscript of Maurice Maeterlinck

By Bernard Miall

Fredonia Books
Amsterdam, The Netherlands

Sister Beatrice

by
Maurice Maeterlinck

ISBN 1-58963-247-8

Translated into English Verse from the Manuscripts
by Bernard Miall

Reprinted from the Original edition

Fredonia Books
Amsterdam, The Netherlands
http://www.fredoniabooks.com

TRANSLATOR'S PREFACE

I

"THESE two little plays,"* says the author, "are really librettos. Music is being written to them by M. Gilkas." The French version is in unrhymed alexandrines, if the term be permissible; that is, in unrhymed lines of twelve syllables. It is of course possible to employ this metre in English verse, but it is a medium as yet too little polished by use to refract, without theft or distortion, its immanent sense; it is, so to speak, one of your material metres, more ready to present itself in body than in spirit, being still in a primitive stage of evolution, and waiting the master-hand which shall teach it an easy delivery and self-effacement. In short, it is a metre neither so far familiar nor so far developed as to justify its use by a translator, whose duty is to interpret his author, in some remote degree, as his author might wish, rather than to experiment as himself might please.

For myself, I had no envy to attempt it, and so, with my author's approval, I have turned his play into such blank verse as I might; holding, with him, that our English unrhymed verse of ten syllables, iambic in scheme,—trochaic, dactylic, anapæstic, catalectic, and what not by incident,—is an equivalent sufficiently near, and perhaps the most proper, of the French unrhymed verse of twelve syllables. But I do not pretend that the author's mood may not be betrayed by the staccato effect of the shorter line. To the French alexandrine, of all metres, is possible at times a

" linkéd sweetness long drawn out,"
which by a shorter metre, or, indeed,
by any metre consisting, as ours, very
largely of accent, is rarely attainable.

Readers may miss in "Sister Beatrice"
what they are used to call the glamour,
the atmosphere, of the Maeterlinckian
drama. They will miss it partly, no
doubt, because I have translated it; but
partly also because it is partly absent
in the French; they may, perhaps, find
more of it in the music, if they have
the fortune to hear it. But the play
unsung, unstaged,—it is, as I have said,
a libretto—is the play of M. Maeterlinck's which most nearly approaches, in
the matter of treatment, the avowedly
obvious spirit of the English drama.
That the story is all spiritual, or rather,
that the spiritual in the play has a story,
is no doubt the reason why the treatment may be material and articulate.

Translator's Preface

Other plays of this author might be described — he himself, I think, might so describe them—as belonging to static or potential drama : the plays were the dramas of a state of feeling. Here, I think, we have for the first time in M. Maeterlinck's theatre the treatment of a legend already crystallised : a legend in England familiar to readers of Mr. John Davidson's poetry in " The Ballad of a Nun." It has also been treated by Miss Adelaide Anne Procter, and a singularly charming translation of the original Dutch version — for in Dutch we find it first told and first printed— may be found in the first volume of a publication called the "Pageant," issued some years ago. This version was translated by Mr. Laurence Housman and Mr. J. Simons ; whether it be the oldest or the original version I am unable to say.

Translator's Preface

This to explain why "Sister Beatrice"
is not most obviously by M. Maeterlinck,
and by no one else.

LIDO, VENICE,
    May 10, 1900.

II

IN translating "Ardiane and Barbe Bleue,"
which, like "Sister Beatrice," was written as
a libretto, I have again used the ordinary
"blank verse" line to represent the unrhymed French line of twelve syllables.
But in the original text of this drama
there are many passages in *vers libre*,
both rhymed and otherwise. To make
irregular metres readable in English re-
quires no less than inspiration, and if
inspiration is not always at the service
of the poet it is still less often at the
beck of the translator. In such passages
I have therefore preserved, so far as

possible, the original measures, but have in all cases, or nearly all, retained or added rhyme.

It was not easy to decide whether I should call our familiar hero-villain Bluebeard or Barbe Bleue. As children we connect him with Ali Baba and the Forty Thieves; but if he be anything less than universal he would appear to be French. Some would relegate him merely to the post of an accidentally baptized variety of the Myth of the Closed Chamber;[1] some identify him with a certain Marshal and Constable of France,[2] companion-in-arms to the Duke of Brittany; some say he is Henry VIII.; at all events one

---

[1] See "The Forbidden Chamber": E. Sidney Hartland, *Folk-lore Journal*, 1885, vol. iii. Also Mr. Lang's edition of Perrault. It was from Perrault that M. Maeterlinck obtained the legend, which he has altered to suit himself.

[2] See "Un Maréchal et un Connétable de France. La Barbe Bleue de la légende et de l'histoire," in the British Museum.

Translator's Preface

Gilles de Lavalle, sieur de Rais, and lord
in all of some eight goodly châteaux,
for the most part in Brittany, constable
and marshal as aforesaid, did commit
certain atrocities upon certain women and
children, though his wife survived him,
and he was in 1440 executed therefor,
at the age of thirty-six. One popular
legend has it that the brothers of seven
deceased wives arrived with Saint Gildas,
whereupon the castle crumbled away, and
the brothers killed the marshal and
constable. Whether this feudal dignitary,
who in his twenties was marshal, constable,
and councillor to King Charles VII., was
or was not the original of the Bluebeard
legend, it is certain that of the ruins of
his numerous castles all are known by
the latter's name, and are connected with
legends of his atrocities; and in one, the
castle of Chantocé, which one Thiphaine
or Triphine d'Anguille gave in 1100 to

the forebears of one Marie de Crain, who in marriage brought it to Gui, father of Rais, father of Barbe Bleue, or Gilles de Lavalle, may be seen to this day a long subterranean hall, communicating with another, low and square, which is entered by three staircases. Chantocé is built on a flat rock, surrounded by a moat, and was defended by two towers with drawbridges. It is interesting to note that the depravity of Gilles was attributed to the fervent study of pernicious literature in his youth.

As the story of Bluebeard pure and simple, as distinguished from that of Bluebeard Gilles, is found in Greek, French, Tuscan, Icelandic, Esthonian, Gaelic, and Basque, it seems unlikely that Gilles was the origin of the legend. It is most likely that the Myth of the Forbidden Chamber found, as all stories will sooner or later find, an exposition in actual life; so that the real drama, in course of years and popular relation, took to itself some or all of the international Forbidden Chamber details, while the Forbidden Chamber stories were given, in many countries, a name, and in France a local habitation—or rather some eight or nine such.

The name of the victorious and final wife is variable. Often it is Anne. Sometimes she finds the corpses, sometimes the heads; the wives, who are usually seven, are sometimes her sisters and sometimes not. Sometimes her brothers kill the polygamous husband; sometimes she has no brothers, and restores the wives to life, as she does in one of the Gaelic versions. In the version of Perrault, which is probably the original of all our English versions, she finds the bodies of the wives, and her brothers execute justice.

Translator's Preface

When I thought of retaining the French name of the hero, it was, as I say, to preserve the reader from reminiscences of the pantomime and the Arabian Nights, which somehow do not " march together " with the drama of M. Maeterlinck. I finally determined to retain " Barbe Bleue " for the name of our hero because the names of all the other characters are French, and untranslatable, and it seemed to me that the contrast of the English name of our hero would still further accentuate the illegitimate Arabian and pantomimic reminiscences that, for some of us, cling to it. Plain " Bluebeard " is hardly congruous with these other names ; we have never thought of our childhood's monster as the warden of a harem of maidens out of a play by M. Maeterlinck. The point is difficult as it is nice, and also trivial, and perhaps it is best to leave the reader to give our hero the name that

his individual taste dictates. My apology
is to disarm the captious.

A word as to the versification of these
two translations. They are for the most
part written in what is popularly called
"blank verse." At the same time, be-
sides employing the slight variations
which precedence allows in such verse, I
have introduced, here and there, what I
conceive to be a variation especially desir-
able in a translation, wherein one cannot
always, or often, choose one's words, and
is sometimes compelled to employ a phrase
that would, if handled in the ordinary
way, be unmusical in the extreme. This
variation consists in the employment of
the well-known principle of catalexis where
not to employ that principle would result
in cacophony. To render certain conca-
tenations of consonants, especially those
containing sibilants, tolerable to the ear, I
have allowed for the time which their

pronunciation actually demands, by counting them as a syllable, so that the decasyllabic line, though still having the time of ten syllables, has only nine syllables in it if estimated in the ordinary way. An example of such a line is :—

" In silence shed before a queen's feet."

Another example is—

" Open the fifth door."—" Not even there ? "

I should not have referred to this matter had not a critic quoted one of the above lines as a proof that I was ignorant of the elementary rules of versification.

BERNARD MIALL.

London, *April* 18, 1901.

* The Preface refers to two plays, as it originally appeared in an edition combining:

Sister Beatrice and *Ardiane & Barbe Bleue*

SISTER BEATRICE

A MIRACLE PLAY IN THREE ACTS

THE PERSONS OF THE PLAY

THE HOLY VIRGIN (in the likeness of
    SISTER BEATRICE)
SISTER BEATRICE
THE ABBESS
SISTER EGLANTINE
SISTER CLEMENCY
SISTER FELICITY
SISTER BALBINA
SISTER REGINA
SISTER GISELA
THE PRIEST
PRINCE BELLIDOR
LITTLE ALLETTE

Beggars, Pilgrims, &c.

TIME—*The Thirteenth Century.* PLACE—*A
Convent in the neighbourhood of Louvain.*

2

SISTER BEATRICE

ACT THE FIRST

*A corridor, in the centre of which is the
great entrance-door of the convent. To
the right, the door of the chapel, to which
a few steps give access, makes an angle
with the wall of the corridor. In the
angle so formed an image of the* VIRGIN,
*of the stature of an ordinary woman,
stands within a niche, on a pedestal of
marble, which is raised on steps and
enclosed within a grille. The image is
attired after the Spanish manner, in
vestments of silk and precious brocades,
which give it the semblance of a celestial
princess. A broad girdle, wrought in*

gold, encircles the waist, and a golden
fillet, on which glitter precious stones,
confines, like a diadem, the tresses of
woman's hair that fall about the
shoulders of the image. To the left
of the convent door is seen the cell of
SISTER BEATRICE. The door of the
cell is ajar. The white-washed cell is
furnished with a chair, a table, and
a pallet-bed. It is night. Before the
VIRGIN a lamp is burning, and at her
feet is prostrated SISTER BEATRICE.

BEATRICE

Pity me, Lady: me about to fall
In mortal sin, for he is coming back
To-night, to-night, and I am alone!
What must I say to him, what must I do?
He looks at me with trembling hands,
    and I—
I know not what it is that he desires.
Since I came first into this holy house

Sister Beatrice

Four years are nearly gone—ay, four years
    quite
But for six weeks, when August meets
    July.
Then I knew nothing: I was quite a
    child:
And now I still know nothing; nor I dare
Ask of the Abbess, nor to any tell
This matter that torments my heart—this
    woe,
Or else, this happiness. It is, they say,
Allowed to love a man in marriage: he,
When first of all I leave the convent, says,
Before he even kiss me, there shall be
A hermit, one who does miraculous things,
One that he knows, who shall unite us
    both.
We are told often of the lures of sin,
And of the snares of man: but him you
    know;
He is not like the others. Long ago,
When I was little, he would often come

Sister Beatrice

Into my father's garden of a Sunday;
We played together there.   Him I forgot,
But oftentimes I would remember that
When I was miserable, or in my prayers.
Pious he is and wise: his eyes are gentler
Than those of a little child that kneels to
    pray.
Here at your feet he knelt the other
    night,
Under the lamp: did you not see him
    there?
To look at, like your Son. Gravely he
    smiles,
As if he spoke to God, though but to me,
To me who cannot answer him he speaks,
Me who have no possessions. See, I tell
    you
All: for I seek not to deceive you: see,
I am very wretched, though for three days
    now
I have been unable to cry any more.
Did I refuse to listen to his prayer

6

Sister Beatrice

He swore that he would die! And I
    have heard
That such a thing may happen; such as
    he,
Men that are beautiful, and tall, and
    young,
Have slain themselves because of love.
    One day
They spoke of this to Francis and to
    Paul.
If this be true I know not: but the earth
Is full of trouble, and they tell us naught.
O Mother, hear! I know not what to
    do!
And who knows, Mother, that these
    trembling hands
Held forth to your holy image shall not
    be
Torches unquenchable in the blaze of Hell
To-morrow?

      [*There is heard without the sound of
         many approaching horsemen.*

Sister Beatrice

> Listen! Listen! Do you hear?
> There are horses — many! Now they
> stop! Ah, now
> Feet on the threshold! now they try the
> door!
>
> [*A knock on the great door.*
>
> What, what to do? Mother, I will not
> go,
> I will not, if you wish it!
>
> [*She rises, and runs to the door.*
>
> Bellidor?

BELLIDOR (*from without*)

Yes, open quickly, Beatrice! it is I!

BEATRICE

Yes, yes!

> [*She throws wide open the door of
> the convent, and* BELLIDOR,
> *clad in a coat of mail and a
> long blue cloak, is seen upon
> the threshold. On his right*

8

*hand is a boy laden with
costly garments and glittering
jewels. Not far from the door
is an old man, who holds two
richly-appointed horses by their
bridles, and leads them to and
fro beneath a tree. In the distance, under the starry sky, a
limitless moonlit country.*

BEATRICE (*advancing*)

You are not alone?   Who is it there,
Under the tree?

BELLIDOR

Draw nigh, and have no fear!
[*Kneeling upon the threshold he kisses
the hem of* BEATRICE'S *robe.*
O, beautiful, as you come forward so,
Beatrice! to front the stars that wait for
you

9

Sister Beatrice

As you upon the threshold trembling
    stand !
Surely they know a mighty happiness
Has come to birth, and, like the dust of
    gold
In silence shed before a queen's feet,
They are strewn over all the long blue ways
We go to travel through. What is it?
    Say !
What would you, what? O, do your feet
    already
Falter? You turn your head? O no,
    no, no !
My arms enlace you, hold you forever
    fast
In the sight of Heaven ! No! you shall
    not fly,
For my enchaining love delivers you !
O come, come, seek no more the shadows
    dim
Of the lamps wherein love slumbered.
    Love has seen

Sister Beatrice

The light he never saw before : the light
Whose every passing ray his triumph gilds,
Unites our youthful spirits, and ensures
Our destinies.   O Beatrice, Beatrice !
Behold, I see you, I am near you, touch,
Embrace you and salute you the first time !

> [*At these words he abruptly rises,*
> *seizes* BEATRICE *about the*
> *body, and kisses her on the lips.*

BEATRICE (*recoiling, and feebly defending*
herself)

No, do not kiss me !   You had promised
me !

BELLIDOR (*redoubling his kisses*)

O, those were never promises of love !
Love cannot say that love will not adore,
And lovers make no promises ; never they
Shall promise aught who once have given
all !
Love every moment gives the all it has,

11

And if it promise to reserve or stay
One kiss, it gives a hundred thousand more
To efface the wrong done to its lips itself.

> [*Embracing her more ardently and
> seeking to draw her away.*

Come, come! The night is passing, and
    the sky
Already paler, and the horses fret.
There is now one step only more to take,
One to descend—

> [*Suddenly observing that* BEATRICE *is
> failing in his arms.*

              You do not answer me?
I do not hear you breathe: your knees
    give way!
Come! Never wait until the envious
    dawn
Outlays its golden snares across the path
That leads to happiness!

    BEATRICE (*who is almost swooning*)
              No, I cannot yet!

Sister Beatrice

BELLIDOR

Love, you grow pale! and all my kisses
    die
Quenched on your lips like sparks in waters
    cold.
Raise your fair face, and give me your
    dear mouth,
That strives to smile no more. Oh! it
    is this,
This heavy veil that so constrains your
    throat,
And weighs upon your heart. 'Twas
    made for death,
Never for life!

> *[With slow and cautious movements
> he unwraps the veil which
> envelops the face of* BEATRICE,
> *who is still unconscious. Pre-
> sently the first tresses of hair
> begin to fall, then others and
> still others, till at last all, like*

13

Sister Beatrice

flames unimprisoned, fall sud-
denly over BEATRICE's *face.*
She seems to awaken.

BELLIDOR (*with a cry of ecstasy*)

O !

BEATRICE (*softly, as if she came from*
a dream)

Ah, what have you done,
Bellidor ? What is this my hands perceive ?
This softness that is tender with my face ?

BELLIDOR (*passionately kissing her*
dishevelled hair)

Behold, behold ! It is your proper fire
Awakens you, and you are overwhelmed
With your own beauty ! Lo, you are
    enmeshed
With your own radiance ! O, you never
    knew,
I never knew, how beautiful you were !

Sister Beatrice

I thought that I had seen you, and I
    thought
I loved you! Ay, and but a moment
    gone
You were the fairest of my boyish dreams :
Most beautiful of all most beautiful
I find you now to my awakened eyes,
And to my hands that touch you, and in
    my heart
That now discovers you!   Ah, wait, wait,
    wait !
You must in all be like your face—must
    be
Utterly liberated, wholly queen !

        [*He removes* BEATRICE'S *mantle with*
          a sudden gesture, and she ap-
          pears clad in a robe of white
          woollen ; then, while he makes
          a sign in the direction of the
          door, and the boy who was
          with him at the opening of the
          scene draws near, bearing costly

*raiment, a golden girdle, and a
necklet of pearls,* BEATRICE *falls
to kneeling on the flags, prostrate and sobbing, her face
hidden in the folds of the
mantle and veil, which she has
gathered up.*

BEATRICE

No, no! I would—I would not!
[*Moving on her knees to the* VIRGIN'S
feet.

O, you see,
Lady! I cannot struggle any more!
No, not without you succour me! I can
pray
No more, no more, if you abandon me!

BELLIDOR (*hastening to* BEATRICE *and
wrapping her in the costly garments
which he has taken from the child*)

It is time, Beatrice! See the raiment, see
The raiment of your life that now begins!

Sister Beatrice

You are no slave I rescue from her lord,
You are a queen I bring to happiness!

BEATRICE (*still kneeling, her hands clinging
    to the grille that encloses the base of
    the image*)

Our Lady, hear me! I can speak no more,
And no more can I any longer pray;
No, I can only sob. I did not know
I loved him quite like this; I did not
    know
That I loved you so much. O listen,
    look!
All that I ask you is a sign, a sign,
A sign of your hand, a smile of your eyes,
    no more!
I am only a girl who does not under-
    stand . . .
They have so often told me that you
    grant
Everything, and that you were very kind,
That you were pitiful . . .

Sister Beatrice

BELLIDOR (*endeavouring to raise her up,
and to draw her gently away from
the grille*)

                          Ay, so she is,
For she is queen of a heaven that love has
     made !
Unclasp these tender hands the iron chills,
Look in her face—it is in no wise wroth,
It smiles, it shines; her eyes have seen
     the prayer
That shines in yours; it is as though
     your tears
Illumed her eyes that smile. Is it not
     she
That asks, and you that pardon? In
     my eyes
You are confounded, and I seem to see
Two sisters, and I know that love is
     here ;
And they bless one another with their
     hands.

18

Sister Beatrice

BEATRICE (*raising her head and looking*
at the VIRGIN)

I was told often I was like her.

BELLIDOR

Look!

Regard, across your own, her tresses, thus,
While so my hands outspread the shim-
    mering veil.
Would you not say, rays of the self-same
    light,
The self-same bliss?
      [*While he speaks three hours are*
        struck on the convent clock.

BEATRICE (*suddenly rising*)

Listen!

BELLIDOR

Three hours!

BEATRICE

The hour

Of matins that I should have sounded!

19

Sister Beatrice

BELLIDOR

Come!
The dawn grows nigh, the windows pale
    to blue!

BEATRICE

The windows I would always open wide
Before the dawn, so might the morning air,
Fresh, and the daylight, and the song of
    birds
Welcome my sisters as they came from
    sleep.
There is the cord that rings the bell to say
Night and their sleep are ended; there
    the door,
The chapel door of which no more my
    hands
Will push apart the leaves to greet the
    dawn,
And altar-candles other hands will light.
Here is the basket of the poor: ay, soon
They will come hither, and will call my
    name,

And see no one at all, and vainly seek
These hands they are wont to bless when
    I dispense
The humble garments that my sisters sew
In peace and silence of the spacious halls
The while they pray . . .

BELLIDOR

        Come, for the day is nigh ;
Your sisters will awaken ; and it seems
Already that I hear their steps re-
    sound . . .

BEATRICE

Ay, they are coming, ay, my sisters come,
Who loved me all so well, and held me too
So holy ! Here will they discover all
That of the lowly Beatrice remains ;
Her veil and mantle lying on the stones.

    [*Suddenly she takes up the veil and
        mantle and deposits them on the
        grille at the feet of the image.*

21

Sister Beatrice

But no; I would never one of them should
    think
I trampled underfoot the robe of peace
They gave me, Mother—see, I give them
    you,
And you will keep them. In your hands
    I place
All my possessions, all that I received
In these four years.

                    I lay my chaplet here,
My chaplet with the cross of silver; here
My discipline, and here the three great
    keys
I carried at my girdle: this the key
That opens the great door; the garden,
    this,
And this, the chapel. I shall see no
    more
The garden growing green, and no more
    now
Unlock the chapel where we used to
    sing

Sister Beatrice

'Mid odour of the incense.   You know all,
Lady, and I know nothing.

                                    There on high
Is it writ that naught is pardoned ?   And
      that love
Is cursed, and that none may expiate it ?
Tell, tell, O tell me ! For I am not
      lost
Except you will it !   I am not now lost
If you but make a sign !   I do not ask
Aught of impossible miracle, only this :
A single sign were all enough ; a sign
So small that none should see it !   If the
      shadow
Cast by the lamp, slumbering on your
      brow,
Move but a line I will not go away !
I will not go away !   O look at me !
Mother !   I gaze and gaze !   I wait !
      [*She gazes for a long while at the*
            VIRGIN's *face.   All is motionless
            and silent.*

Sister Beatrice

BELLIDOR (*embracing her and kissing her passionately on the lips*)

Come!

BEATRICE (*for the first time returning his kiss*)

Yes!

[*Enlaced in one another's arms, they go forth into the dawning world. The door is left open. Soon is heard the sound of horses that gallop away away into the distance. The curtain falls, and shortly afterwards the bell of the convent is heard in the dawn, loudly ringing matins.*

END OF THE FIRST ACT

24

ACT THE SECOND

The last strokes of the bell ringing matins are heard. Then the curtain rises. The scene is that of the last Act, save that now the great door of the convent is closed, and all the corridor windows are open to the first rays of the sun. Hardly has the curtain risen when the VIRGIN, *as at the end of a long, divine sleep, is seen to stir, to come to life; then slowly she descends the steps of the pedestal, and reaches the grille, and over her glorious robe and tresses she puts on the veil and mantle that* BEATRICE *has abandoned. Then, as she begins to sing softly under her breath, she turns to the right, stretching forth her hand, when, through the door*

Sister Beatrice

*of the chapel, which opens to her
gesture, are seen the tapers of the
altar ; which are magically one by
one being kindled ; then, continuing
her holy song, she revives the flame of
the lamp, and having placed before the
pedestal the basket which contains the
garments to be given to the poor, she
advances to the great door of the
convent.*

THE VIRGIN (*singing*)

I hold to every sin,
   To every soul that weeps,
My hands with pardon filled
   Out of the starry deeps.

There is no sin that lives
   If love have vigil kept ;
There is no soul that dies
   If love but once have wept.

26

Sister Beatrice

And though in many paths
  Of earth love lose its way,
Its tears shall find me out,
  And shall not go astray.

*[During the last words of the song a
hand knocks timidly at the
gate of the convent. The
VIRGIN opens; and there appears on the threshold a little
girl, barefooted, and very ragged
and poor. She is half hidden
behind the oaken door-post;
she advances only her head, and
gazes at the VIRGIN with as-
tonishment.*

THE VIRGIN

Good day, Allette, why do you hide
  yourself?

*[Enraptured and afraid, making the
sign of the cross as she approaches.*

27

Sister Beatrice

ALLETTE

Why have you put that light upon your
 robe ?

THE VIRGIN

After the dawn there is light everywhere.

ALLETTE

Why have you put those stars into your
 eyes ?

THE VIRGIN

There are often stars in the depth of eyes
 that pray.

ALLETTE

Why have you put that light inside your
 hands?

THE VIRGIN

There is always light in the hands of alms-
 givers.

ALLETTE

I have come alone here.

Sister Beatrice

THE VIRGIN

Where are our poor brothers?

ALLETTE

They dare not come because of what folk
say.

THE VIRGIN

What do they say?

ALLETTE

They say that they have seen
Beatrice riding on the Prince's horse.

THE VIRGIN

Am I not like the lowly Beatrice?

ALLETTE

They say they have seen her—that she
spoke to them.

THE VIRGIN

Only God saw her not, and nothing heard.
  [*Taking the child in her arms and
  kissing her on the forehead.*

29

Sister Beatrice

O little one, Allette, there is no one else
To-day that I can kiss.   Ay, innocence
Cannot betray me, though it comprehend.
            [*Looking into the child's eyes.*
How pure the human soul when thus one
        sees it !
Most beautiful the angels are, but they
Never know tears.   Poor child, enough,
        enough !
Behold yours falling; you shall know
        their number !
   [*She sets the child down on the threshold.*
But our poor brothers—where are they?
        Allette,
Go forth to them, and tell them all of
        love
Full of impatience : go, and bid them
        haste.

ALLETTE (*who turns her head and looks
        away from the convent*)

O Sister Beatrice, they are coming—see !

30

Sister Beatrice

[*And indeed the poor, the sick and
infirm, the women carrying
little children, have timidly
drawn nigh, and, thinking that
they recognise* Beatrice, *fearful, hesitating, and astonished,
they approach the threshold,
and, halting outside the door,
they gaze and wait.*

The Virgin (*leaning over the poor-basket,
which contains clothes*)

What has befallen? Brothers, wherefore
stay?
Hasten! the sun already mounts: the
time
Is ripe for prayer; shortly my sisters pass.
The door will soon be shut; then, till the
morrow,
No more of alms. O come you, all of
you!
O hasten, all of you; the time is now.

31

Sister Beatrice

A POOR OLD MAN (*coming forward*)

Now, sister, we to-night have seen two
    ghosts . . .

THE VIRGIN (*giving him a cloak, which
    suddenly becomes radiant as she draws
    it out of the basket*)

Dream now no more of phantoms of the
    night.

A CRIPPLE (*advancing in turn*)

We have had wicked thoughts this night,
    my sister.

THE VIRGIN (*drawing from the basket
    another garment, which seems suddenly
    to become covered with jewels*)

Open your eyes, my brother : it is now
The hour of pardon. Come, O all of
    you, come !

32

Sister Beatrice

A Poor Woman

I, sister, for my mother need a shroud . . .

Another Poor Woman

I beg you, sister, that our latest-born . . .

> [*The poor folk, lamenting, and
> greedy of charity, their arms
> outheld, press in a crowd about
> the* Virgin, *who, leaning over
> the basket, fills her arms from
> it again and again with gar-
> ments glittering with rays of
> light, sparkling veils, and robes
> of linen that grow luminous.
> In measure as the* Virgin
> *exhausts the basket it over-
> flows with a still greater abun-
> dance of raiment, more and
> more costly, and more and
> more resplendent ; and as
> though intoxicated by the*

Sister Beatrice

miracle she herself has worked,
she cries out, as she distributes
her treasures to the poor folk,
filling their hands, covering
their shoulders, and wrapping
their infants in dazzling and
blazing tissues.

THE VIRGIN

O come you hither, hither, all of you
    come!
The snowy shroud is here, and here behold
The smiling swaddling-bands! Ay, here
    behold
Life, death, and life again! Come hither
    all!
It is the hour of love: and what of love?
It has no limits! Come you, all of you,
    come!
Give one another aid! and all offence
Let each forgive the other! And through
    life

34

Sister Beatrice

Mingle your happinesses and your tears!
Love one another: pray for those that
    fall:
Come all, come hither, all of you pass by!
Come, all of you! God does not see the
    ill
Done without hatred. Pardon one another:
There is no sin forgiveness does not reach.

> [*Now the poor people, stupefied and
> bewildered, are covered with
> resplendent garments. Some,
> their raiment rustling with
> precious stones, waving and
> swaying as they go, flee into
> the open, shouting for joy.
> Others, sobbing for gratitude,
> surround the holy* VIRGIN, *and
> seek to kiss her hands. But
> the greater number, silent, and
> as though smitten with a divine
> terror, kneel upon the steps of
> the entrance and murmur their*

*prayers. Then a stroke of the
bell is heard; the basket is
suddenly exhausted; the Virgin gently disperses the poor
folk who press about her, and
closes the door on them.*

The Virgin

Go in peace, brethren : 'tis the hour of
    prayer.

        *[The murmur of the poor folk at
        prayer is still heard through
        the closed door. The murmur
        little by little becomes an indis-
        tinct hymn of gratitude and
        ecstasy. A second, then a third
        stroke of the bell resounds ; and
        proceeding from the left end of
        the corridor the Nuns, with
        the Abbess at their head, ad-
        vance toward the chapel.*

Sister Beatrice

THE ABBESS (*halting before the* VIRGIN, *who, with bended head, and hands disposed upon her breast, waits by the closed door*)

Hear, Sister Beatrice. This month of sun
Matins are rung a quarter short of three.
Now you shall three days fast, shall three
      nights pray
Before the Virgin's feet that was a
    mother.

THE VIRGIN (*bowing with the humblest gestures of assent*)

My Mother, God be praised!
      [THE ABBESS, *resuming her steps,*
      reaches the pedestal, which be-
      fore was hidden from her by
      the wall from which springs the
      vaulting of the great doorway.
      There she is about to kneel,
      when, upon raising her eyes,

*she stops, cries aloud, lets fall
the book that she carries, and
makes a gesture of unspeakable
surprise and horror.*

THE ABBESS

         She is not there!
[*Disquieted, then terrified, the* NUNS
run to the ABBESS, *surrounding
her and crowding about the
pedestal. The first moment of
stupefaction having passed, they
all speak, cry aloud, moan, and
lament at the same moment, by
turns outraged, terrified, sobbing, upright, kneeling, prostrated, or staggering.*

THE NUNS

She is no longer there!
            The Virgin gone!
Her image has been stolen!
           Infidels!

Sister Beatrice

Our Mother, O our Mother!

> Sacrilege!

The cloister is profaned!

> O Sacrilege!

The roof will fall upon us!

> Sacrilege!

Sacrilege!

> Sacrilege!
>
> > Sacrilege!

THE ABBESS (*calling aloud*)

> Sister Beatrice!

[*The* VIRGIN *advances, and halts before the pedestal, close to the* ABBESS. *She gazes fixedly at the spot where her image used to stand, and her impassive eyes and face, as though sealed from the outer world, are, as it were, radiant with an imperturbable hope and silence.*

Sister Beatrice

THE ABBESS

You, Sister Beatrice, were she in charge,
And it was yours by day or night to wake
And watch above the majesty of her
Who made this convent-house her treasury
Of graces, and to house her predilections:
I understand your anguish, and your fear
I share. Yet fear you naught! The
    Will Divine
Has oftentimes designs that must con-
    found
Our vigilance and zeal.   But answer me;
Speak, for you must have seen; speak,
    you must know!

                    [*The* VIRGIN *is silent.*
Answer me! Speak! What is amiss
    with you?
It seems to me there is somewhat strange
    —it seems
At moments that your face grows
    radiant . . .

And say, what are these garments, now
    no more
The same as all we wear? Why, do my
    eyes
Deceive me? One that looks at you
    would say
You are no more the same. What have
    you there,
There, there, beneath your mantle, this
    that gleams
So brightly through it?

          [*She feels the* VIRGIN's *mantle.*

              Ay, and what this stuff
Whose folds translucent run ablaze with
    light,
When my hands touch it?

         [*She opens the* VIRGIN's *mantle, and be-*
           holds the girdle of wrought gold.

              Mercy! What is this?

         [*She removes the mantle entirely, and*
           in the same moment of out-
           raged stupefaction she snatches

Sister Beatrice

off the veil which covers the VIRGIN'S *hair, and the latter, always motionless, and as though insensible, appears suddenly clothed after the manner of and exactly in all points resembling her image that occupied the pedestal during the First Act. At this spectacle there falls on the* ABBESS *and the* NUNS *who crowd round her a moment of silent stupefaction and incredulous anguish. Then the* ABBESS, *who is the first to regain control over herself, covers her face with a gesture of despairing horror and malediction, and cries :*

Lord God !

THE NUNS

Our Lady ! She has robbed the image ! Speak, Sister Beatrice !

Sister Beatrice

She does not answer!
The Demons!   O, the Demons!
Beware the walls!
They will avenge themselves!
O madness, madness!
O horror, horror!   Let us not await
The thunder-bolt!   O sacrilege, sacrilege!
Sacrilege!   Sacrilege!

*[There is a movement of recoil, terror,
and flight among the* Nuns; *but
the* Abbess *restrains them, raising
her hands and her voice.*

The Abbess

Listen all, my daughters!
Nay, do not fly!   Let us await our lot;
Let us not separate; let all our hands
And all our prayers hedge in the sacrilege,
And strive to appease the ensuing wrath!

Sister Clemency

I pray,
Mother, you will not tarry!

Sister Beatrice

SISTER FELICITY

                              Let us go
To find the priest !

SISTER CLEMENCY

                       I saw him passing by
Deep in the chapel.

THE ABBESS

                    You are right ; yes, go,
Sisters Felicity and Clemency.
Go quickly ; yes, go quickly ; he will know
Better than we what should be done to
        stay,
If yet it be not all too late to stay,
The sword of the Archangel, and to foil
The triumph of the Accursèd One. Ah
        me !
My sisters, my poor sisters ! Horror has
A name no longer, and our eyes have
        plumbed
Ths deepest abysms of hell !

44

Sister Beatrice

SISTER GISELA (*approaching the* VIRGIN)
Profanatrix!

SISTER BALBINA (*also approaching her*)
Sacrilege! Sacrilege!

SISTER REGINA (*beside herself*)
Demon! Demon! Demon!

SISTER EGLANTINE (*in a mournful and
very gentle voice*)
O, Sister Beatrice, what have you done?
[*At the sound of this voice the
VIRGIN turns her head, and
looks at SISTER EGLANTINE
with a smile of divine sweetness.*

SISTER BALBINA (*to* SISTER EGLANTINE)
She looks at you.

45

Sister Beatrice

SISTER GISELA

She seems to awake.

SISTER EGLANTINE

Perhaps
You did not know—

THE ABBESS

No, Sister Eglantine,
I will not have you speak to her!
[*At this moment the* PRIEST, *wear-
ing his priestly appointments,
appears at the door of the
chapel, followed by two* NUNS
and the terrified Choristers.

THE PRIEST

Pray, pray!
My sisters, pray for her!

THE ABBESS (*throwing herself on
her knees*)

You know, my father . . .

46

Sister Beatrice

THE PRIEST (*in a stern voice*)

Hear, Sister Beatrice!
      [*The* VIRGIN *remains motionless.*

THE PRIEST (*in a loud voice*)

                  Sister Beatrice!
      [*The* VIRGIN *remains motionless.*

THE PRIEST (*in a terrible voice*)

Hear, Sister Beatrice!   Now, for the third
    time
I call you, in the name of the living God,
Whose anger trembles round about these
    walls—
I call you by your name!

THE ABBESS

               She does not hear!

SISTER REGINA

She does not wish to hear!

47

Sister Beatrice

SISTER BALBINA

            O misery
O woe to all of us!

SISTER GISELA

          Father! Intercede!
Have pity on us!

THE PRIEST

          Doubt is at an end.
Now do I recognise the gloomy pride
Of the Prince of Darkness and the Father
    of Pride.

          [*Turning to the* ABBESS.
My sister, I deliver her to you,
And mark that man's indulgence nowise
    may
Cheat the prerogatives of Love Divine.
Go, go, my sisters; drag the culprit forth
To the foot of the holy altars; then tear
    off,

Sister Beatrice

There, in the presence of that One to
    whom
The angels bow—there tear off, one by
    one,
The vestments and the gems of sacri-
    lege.
Unloose your girdles ; every scourge twist
    tight,
And from the pillars of the portal
    take
The heavy lashes of prevaricators,
And rods of grievous penance. May
    your arms
Be cruel, may your hands be pitiless !
Mercy it is that lends them strength, and
    Love
That blesses them ! Go forth, my sisters,
    go!

      [*The* Nuns *drag the* Virgin *away.*
        She walks indifferent in their
        midst, docile and impassive.
        All, save Sister Eglantine,

*have already untied the double-
knotted cords which gird their
loins. They enter the chapel,
and the doors close ; only the
PRIEST remains, and bows himself before the forsaken pedestal.
There is for some time silence.
Suddenly a song of unspeakable
sweetness filters through the
doors of the chapel. It is the
sacred canticle of the VIRGIN,
the Ave Maris Stella, which
sounds as though sung by the
distant voices of angels. Little
by little the hymn becomes more
distinct, draws near, grows
fuller, becomes universal, as
though an invisible host, ever
more and more innumerable,
took it up with a might ever
more and more ardent, ever
more and more celestial. At*

the same time there is heard from within the chapel the sound of seats overturned, of candelabras falling, of stalls thrown into confusion, and the exclamations of terrified human voices. Finally the two leaves of the door are violently thrown wide, and the nave appears all inundated with flames and strange splendours, which undulate, blossom forth, gyrate, and sweep past one another, infinitely more dazzling than the splendour of the sun whose rays light the corridor. Then, amid the delirious Alleluias and Hosannas which burst forth on every hand—confounded, haggard, transfigured, mad with joy and superhuman awe, waving armsful of blossoming boughs

5 1

that overflow with miraculous flowers which increase their ecstasy, enveloped from head to foot in living garlands which fetter their steps, blinded by the rain of flower-petals which stream from the vaulting—the NUNS *tumultuously surge into the too narrow doorway, and uncertainly descend the steps, encumbered by the marvellous showers ; and while at each step they strip their burdens of their flowers, only to see them renewing themselves in their hands, they surround the ancient* PRIEST, *who now again stands upright, those that follow advancing in turn through the billows of blossoms that surge continually over the steps of the chapel-door.*

Sister Beatrice

THE NUNS (*all together and on every hand,
    while they emerge from the chapel, fill
    the corridor, singing and embracing one
    another amid the deluge of flowers*)
A miracle!
                A miracle!
                                A miracle!
My father, O, my father!
                                I am blind!
My father, O, my father!
                                A miracle!
Hosanna!
            O, Hosanna!
                                O, the Lord
Is close about us!   O, the Heavens are
    open!
The angels overwhelm us, and the flowers
Pursue us!   Hosanna!   Hosanna!   Sister
    Beatrice
Is holy!   Ring the bell, O peal the bell,
Until the bronze be shattered!   She is holy!
Ah, Sister Beatrice is holy, holy!

Sister Beatrice

SISTER REGINA

I sought to touch her holy vestments.
Then—

SISTER EGLANTINE (*crowned with flowers more radiant than the rest*)

The flames brake forth, the shafts of
light spoke !

SISTER CLEMENCY

The angels of the altars toward us turned !

SISTER GISELA

The saints bowed over her, and joined their
hands !

SISTER EGLANTINE

And all the statues of the pillars knelt !

54

Sister Beatrice

SISTER FELICITY

The archangels all their wings unfurled
    and sang!

SISTER GISELA (*waving heavy garlands
        of roses*)

And living roses brake her bonds in twain!

SISTER BALBINA (*waving enormous stems
        of lilies*)

Miraculous lilies blossomed on the rods!

SISTER FELICITY (*waving luminous
        palm-branches*)

The lashes blazed into long golden palms!

THE ABBESS (*kneeling at the feet of
        the* PRIEST)

My father, O my father, I have sinned.
For Sister Beatrice is holy!

55

Sister Beatrice

THE PRIEST (*kneeling also*)

Yea!

My daughters, yea, my daughters, I have
  sinned!

Behold the ways of God past finding
  out!

> [*At this moment there is heard a
> knock on the entrance-door of
> the convent, and the* VIRGIN,
> *once more human of aspect, and
> humbly clad in the mantle and
> veil of* BEATRICE, *appears in the
> threshold of the chapel. She
> descends the steps, her eyes
> downcast and her hands folded
> together, passes among her kneel-
> ing sisters, over the flowers,
> which stand erect as she goes,
> and resuming, as if nothing had
> happened, the duties of her
> charge, she goes to the door and*

56

Sister Beatrice

*throws it open wide. Three
pilgrims enter, poor, old, and
haggard, to whom she bows low,
and taking from a tripod of
bronze near by the aspergus and
the basin of silver, she sprinkles
the water over their ponderous
hands in silence.*

THE END OF THE SECOND ACT

ACT THE THIRD

The scene is the same. On the pedestal the image of the VIRGIN *stands, as in the First Act ; the veil, mantle, and keys of* SISTER BEATRICE *are hanging on the grille ; the chapel-door is open, and the candles of the altar are lit ; the lamp is burning before the image, and the poor-basket overflows with clothing: in a word, all is precisely as it was at the moment when the* NUN *fled with* PRINCE BELLIDOR, *except that the entrance-door of the convent is now closed. It is early dawn in winter ; the last strokes of matins are heard, though no one rings the bell, and in the porch of the chapel the bell-rope is seen to rise and fall in empty air. Then,*

*the bell having ceased to sound, a
silence falls, which is broken by three
blows struck slowly on the convent door.
At the third blow the door moves without sound on its hinges, though no one
opens it ; and the two leaves are thrown
wide open on the white, desolate, vacant
countryside ; and, amid the whirling
of the snow which drives upon the
threshold there advances, haggard, thin,
and unrecognisable, she who was once*
Sister Beatrice. *She is covered with
rags ; her hair, already grey, is
scattered over her face, which is
grievously pinched and livid. Her
eyes, bruised and black, have in them
only the remote and impassive gaze of
those who are about to die, and hold no
longer any shadow of hope. She halts
a moment in the open doorway, and
then, as she beholds no one, she enters,
swaying, groping, and leaning on the*

Sister Beatrice

doors, sweeping the corridor with her eyes, with the uneasiness of an animal long hunted. But the corridor is empty, and she takes a few more fearful steps, until, perceiving the image of the VIRGIN, *she gives a cry, in which are mingled who shall say what vain and weary hopes of deliverance? — and throws herself, kneeling and fainting, at the feet of the statue.*

BEATRICE

My Mother, I am here! Repulse me
    not,
For you are all I have now in the world!
I hoped that I should see you once again,
And I have come too late, because my
    eyes
Are closing: I no longer see you smile;
And when I stretch my hands out after
    you

Sister Beatrice

I feel they are dead. I have forgotten
    how
To pray, I have forgotten how to speak,
And—since I needs must tell you every-
    thing—
I have wept so many tears that long ago
I lost all heart ever to cry again.
Forgive me, O forgive me, if I speak
A name that never should again be heard:
You would not recognise your daughter
    else.

O see to what estate have brought her
    love,
And sin, and all that men call happiness!
I left you more than twenty years ago;
And if so be 'tis not the will of God
Men should be happy, surely then to me
He should intend no ill, for happy—O,
I have not been that! Thus I to-day
    return,
But ask for nothing, for the hour is gone,
And to receive I have no longer strength.

Sister Beatrice

I come to die here in this holy house,
If but my sisters will permit that I
Fall where I fall. O, never doubt, they
    know !
The scandal of my life has been so
    great
Down yonder in the town, they will have
    heard . . .
But they, they know so little ; even you,
You who know all things, you will never
    know
The wickedness that they have made me
    do,
And all that I have suffered.
                     I would fain
Tell them to all, the agonies of love !
                 [Looking around her.
But why am I alone ?   Lo, all the house
Is void as though my sins had emptied
    it . . .
O, who has taken up the place I fled,
My place before the holy altars, who ?

Sister Beatrice

Who guards the threshold that my feet
    have soiled ?
The lamp is lit: I see the tapers shine ;
Matins have rung, and here behold the
    day
That grows, and none appears.

> *[Perceiving the mantle and veil
> that hung upon the grille.*

                But what is here?

> *[She raises herself a little, draws
> nearer on her knees, and feels the
> veil and mantle.*

Already my poor hands are so near death
They know no longer if the things they
    touch
Are things of this life or the other
    world :
But is not this the mantle that I left . . .
Yesterday . . . five - and - twenty years
    ago ?

> *[Taking up the mantle and mechani-
> cally putting it on.*

Sister Beatrice

It seems the shape—and yet seems very
    long.
When I was happy, when I went erect,
It fitted well enough.

                   [Taking the veil.
                Now the long veil,
That now shall be my winding-sheet. O
    Mother,
Forgive me if it be a sacrilege !
I am cold, I am naked ; for my wretched
    clothes
No longer know my body how to hide,
That knows no longer where to hide itself.
Was it not you, my Mother, kept them
    safe,
Is it not you who give them to me now
Against the hour redoubtable, that thus
The pitiless flames that wait me may per-
    haps
A little hesitate and be less cruel ?

       *[A sound of steps and of opening
          doors is heard.*

Sister Beatrice

What do I hear?

>   [*Three strokes of the bell resound,
>   announcing, as before, the
>   arrival of the* NUNS *in the
>   corridor.*

>   What do I hear?   O Mother!

The   door   swings   open,   and   my   sisters
    come!

I cannot!   Never!   O, have pity, pity!

For the walls crush me, the light suffocates,

And   shame,   shame,   shame,   is   graven   on
    the stones

That rise up, up against me!   Ah!   Ah!
    Ah!

>   [*She falls fainting at the feet of the
>   image. The* NUNS, *preceded
>   by the* ABBESS, *advance along
>   the vaulted passage, as in the
>   preceding Act, on their way to
>   the chapel. Many of them are
>   very old; and the* ABBESS
>   walks painfully, bent double,*

Sister Beatrice

*supporting herself on a staff.
Scarcely have they entered but
they perceive* BEATRICE *lying
motionless across the corridor;
they run to her and crowd
about her, uneasy, frightened,
and dismayed.*

THE ABBESS (*who first sees her*)
O, Sister Beatrice is dead!

SISTER CLEMENCY
                              The Heavens
Gave her, the Lord has taken her away!

SISTER FELICITY
Her crown was ready, and the angels called.

SISTER EGLANTINE (*raising and supporting the head of* SISTER BEATRICE,
*which she kisses with a kind of pious
awe*)

No, no, she is not dead: she shudders,
breathes!

66

Sister Beatrice

But look, how pale she is !   But see, how
   thin !

SISTER CLEMENCY

As though one night had aged her ten
   long years !

SISTER FELICITY

She must have suffered, striving, till the
   dawn !

SISTER CLEMENCY

And all alone against the angelic host
That sought to draw her hence !

SISTER EGLANTINE

                    She suffered much
Already yesternight ; she trembled, wept,
Who, ever since the miracle of flowers,
Nursed in her eyes that smile miraculous.
She would not have me take her place ;
   she said

67

Sister Beatrice

"I wait," she said, "until my saint returns."

SISTER BALBINA

What saint?

        [*The* ABBESS, *raising her eyes at hazard, sees the image of the* VIRGIN *re-established in the pedestal. The* NUNS *raise their heads, and, with the exception of* SISTER EGLANTINE, *who continues to hold the fainting form of* BEATRICE *in her arms, they all turn with cries of ecstasy and throw themselves on their knees at the foot of the pedestal.*

THE NUNS

The Virgin has returned! Our Lady!
Our Mother is saved! And she has all
    her jewels!
Her crown is brighter, and her eyes more
    deep,

68

Sister Beatrice

And sweeter her regard! She has come
    back
From Heaven, and brought Heaven back
    again to us!
Yea, on the wings of her most holy
    prayers . . .

Sister Eglantine

Come, come! I hear her heart no longer!
    Come!
      [*The* Nuns *turn and once more
      crowd about* Beatrice.

Sister Clemency (*kneeling near her*)

Ah, Sister Beatrice, you shall not leave
Your sisters on this high miraculous day!

Sister Felicity

The Virgin smiles on you; her lips appeal!

Sister Eglantine

Alas, she cannot hear! She seems to suffer;
Her face grows hollow—

69

Sister Beatrice

SISTER CLEMENCY

        Bear her to her bed.
Come, let us bear her yonder to her cell.

SISTER EGLANTINE

No : let us rather leave her nigh to Her
Who loves and fences her with miracles.

> [*The* NUNS *enter the cell, returning*
> *with cloaks and linen sheets,*
> *on which they lay* BEATRICE
> *at the feet of the statue.*

SISTER CLEMENCY

She cannot breathe—undo her veil and
    mantle.

> [*She does as she advises, and the*
> NUNS *behold* BEATRICE *covered*
> *with rags.*

SISTER FELICITY

My Mother, have you seen her dripping
    rags ?

SISTER BALBINA

O, she is quite benumbed with melting snow!

70

Sister Beatrice

SISTER CLEMENCY

We never knew her hair had grown so
white.

SISTER FELICITY

Her naked feet are soiled with wayside
mire !

THE ABBESS

Hold we our peace, my daughters; for
we live

Near heaven; the hands that touch her
will remain

Luminous.

SISTER EGLANTINE

See, her breast is heaving !   See !
Her eyes are going to open !

[BEATRICE *opens her eyes, moves her
head a little, and gazes about her.*

BEATRICE (*as though emerging from a
dream, and still bewildered, in a remote voice*)

When they died—

71

Sister Beatrice

My children—when they died. . . . Why
    do you smile?
They died of want.

The Abbess

      We do not smile; we are glad,
Ay, glad to see you coming back to life.

Beatrice

I, coming back to life!
   [*Looking about her with advancing
     recognition.*
          Yes, I remember,
I came here in the depth of my distress.
Look on me not so fearfully: I no more
Shall be the butt of scandal: you shall now
Have all your will of me. No, none
    shall know,
If you should fear that any should ever
    tell—
I shall say nothing. I submit to all,
For they have broken all my body and
    soul.

Sister Beatrice

I know it cannot be allowed that I,
Here in this place, and at the Virgin's feet,
So near the chapel, and so near to all
That holy is and pure, should die. You
    are all,
O, very good ; you have been patient ;
    yes ;
You have not cast me out of doors at once.
But if you may, if God allow it too,
O, do not cast me forth too far from here !
There is no need that any tend me now,
No need that any me commiserate,
Though I am very sick, I suffer now
No more, no more. . . . Why have you
    laid me here,
On these fair sheets of white ? Alas !
    white sheets
Are nothing to me now but a reproach,
And straw polluted is the fitting bed
Of dying sin. But you still look at me,
And still say nothing. And you do not
    look

Sister Beatrice

Angry. I see tears in your eyes. I think
You do not know me yet.

THE ABBESS (*kissing her hands*)

But yes, yes, yes!
Surely we know you, surely—you, our
saint!

BEATRICE (*snatching away her hands in
a kind of terror*)

Kiss not these hands—they have done so
much ill!

SISTER CLEMENCY (*kissing her feet*)

O soul elect come down to us from heaven!

BEATRICE

Kiss not these feet that used to run to sin!

SISTER EGLANTINE (*kissing her forehead*)

I kiss this pure brow, crowned with
miracles.

74

Sister Beatrice

BEATRICE (*hiding her face in her hands*)

What would you all ?   What has befallen ?
    Once,
When I was happy, one was never
    pardoned ;
Kiss not this brow : it has been friends
    with lust !
But you that touched it, tell me who
    you are ?
I am not certain if my weary eyes
Betray me ; but if they see yonder still,
You are Sister Eglantine.

SISTER EGLANTINE

                    Yes, I am she.
That Sister Eglantine whom you have
    loved.

BEATRICE

You, five-and-twenty years ago, I told
I was unhappy.

Sister Beatrice

SISTER EGLANTINE

     Five-and-twenty years
Since, among all our sisters, God chose
 you.
    BEATRICE

You tell me that, and no least bitterness
Lurks in your voice. What has befallen
 me
I cannot fathom.   I am weak and ill,
And cannot recollect—and every word
Astounds me. I was inattentive. See,
I think that you deceive yourselves. I
 am—
Cover your faces, make the holy sign!—
I am Sister Beatrice!

   THE ABBESS

     But yes, we know!
Our Sister Beatrice, our sister, ours,
Purest among us, the miraculous lamb,
Godchild of angels, the immaculate flame!

Sister Beatrice

BEATRICE

Ah, is it truly you? I did not know.
Mother, you used to go so upright; now
How you do stoop! I have also learned
    to stoop,
And now behold me fallen. Yes, I know
All of you : there is Sister Clemency.

SISTER CLEMENCY (*bending her head
      and smiling*)

Yes, yes.

BEATRICE

Sister Felicity.

SISTER FELICITY (*smiling*)
                It is.
Sister Felicity who came the first
Out of the blossoming chapel.

BEATRICE
              And I think
You have not suffered, for you seem not
    sad.
I was the younger : I am the elder now.

77

Sister Beatrice

The Abbess

That is no doubt because of love divine
Being a terrible burden.

Beatrice

                Mother, no.
It is the love of man that is the burden,
The weary burden.　You do pardon me,
You also pardon me?

The Abbess (*kneeling at* Beatrice's *feet*)

                O daughter mine,
If any have need of pardon, it is she
Who can at last prostrate herself before
Your feet.

Beatrice

But do you know what I have done?

The Abbess

You have done naught but miracle, have
    been,

Sister Beatrice

Since the great day of flowers, our soul's
    light,
The incense of our prayers, and the source
Of grace, the gate of marvels!

BEATRICE

But I fled
One night, now five-and-twenty years ago,
With the Prince Bellidor.

THE ABBESS

Of whom do you speak,
Of whom do you speak, my daughter?

BEATRICE

Of myself!
I say myself! You will not understand?
One evening, five-and-twenty years ago,
I fled, and when three months were at an
    end
He did not love me. Then I lost all
    shame,
I lost all reason, and I lost all hope.

79

Sister Beatrice

All men by turns this body have profaned,
This clay to its God unfaithful. And I
    took
Pleasure in this, and called men after me.
I fell so low that Heaven's angels thence
Could not have risen for all their mighty
    wings.
So many crimes I have committed, I
Have often even sin itself defiled !

THE ABBESS (*gently placing her hand on*
    BEATRICE'S *lips*)
Daughter, the Shadow tempts you ; speak
    no more,
For rising anguish robs you of yourself.

SISTER CLEMENCY
She is worn out with miracle.

SISTER FELICITY
                And grace
Confounds her.

Sister Beatrice

SISTER EGLANTINE
The air of heaven weighs her down.

BEATRICE (*who struggles, pushes away the
hand of the* ABBESS *and sits up*)
I do not wander! No, I tell you, no!
This is no air of heaven, but of earth,
And this is truth! Ah, you are all too
mild!
You are too soft and imperturbable!
And you know nothing! I would rather
far
You should afflict me, but should learn at
last!
O, you live here and do your penances,
And say your prayers, and seek to expiate
sin,
But look you, it is I, and all my kind,
Who live beyond the pale and have no
rest,
That do the bitterest penance to the end!

Sister Beatrice

ABBESS

Pray, pray, my sisters; now the final trial!

SISTER EGLANTINE

The triumph of the angels irks the Fiend!

BEATRICE

Yes, yes, it is the Fiend, the Fiend prevails!
See you these hands?   They have a human
        shape
No longer; see, they cannot open now.
I had to sell them after soul and body.
They buy hands also when no more is left.

THE ABBESS (*wiping the sweat from
        BEATRICE's face*)

May Heaven's angels, who about thy
        couch
Now watch thee, deign before thy stream-
        ing face
To spread their wings!

82

Sister Beatrice

            Ah! Heaven's angels! Ah!
Where are they, tell me, and what do
    they do?
Have I not told you? Why, I have not now
My children, for the three most lovely died
When I no more was lovely, and the last,
Lest it should suffer, being one night mad,
I killed. And there were others never born,
Although they cried for birth. And still
    the sun
Shone, and the stars returned, and justice
    slept,
And only the most evil were happy and
    proud.

THE ABBESS

The strife is terrible about great saints.

SISTER EGLANTINE

It is at Heaven's gates the infernal fire
Wastes the huge angers of its futile rage

Sister Beatrice

BEATRICE (*falling back exhausted*)

I care no more—I stifle—what you will
Be done to me.   I had to tell you all.

SISTER EGLANTINE

The archangels bear her forth.

SISTER FELICITY

                The phalanxes
Of the celestial host have brought back
    peace.

THE ABBESS

The evil dream has fled.   Now smile
    again,
My poor and holy sister, while you think
On all the blasphemies you did not speak.
A baneful voice usurping on your lips
Exhaled them in the rage of final loss.

BEATRICE

It was my voice.

Sister Beatrice

THE ABBESS

        My good and holy sister,
Assure your heart, and have you no regrets.
For that was not the voice that all we
      know,
The dear and gentle voice, the angel's pilot,
The health of sickness, that so many years
Quickened our prayers.

SISTER EGLANTINE

         Fear nothing, sister ; nay,
In the last conflict you shall never lose
The palm and diadem of a life of love,
And innocence, and prayer.

BEATRICE

           Never one hour
Since that unhappy hour, in all my life,
There never was an hour that was not
      marked
By mortal sin.

Sister Beatrice

THE ABBESS

My daughter, pray to God!
You are most holy; yet the enemy
Tempts you, and scruples lead your sense
astray.
How should you have committed all these
sins
So dreadful? It is nigh on thirty years
You have been here, of threshold and of
altar
Most humble servitor: my very eyes
Have followed you in all your deeds and
prayers,
And I can answer before God for them
As I would for my own. But would to
Heaven
That mine were like to yours! It is not
here,
Within these cloisters, but without, beyond,
Out in the world estrayed, that sin
triumphs:

Sister Beatrice

And of that world, all thanks to God, you
    know
Nothing, for never have you issued forth
Out of the shadow of the sanctuary.

BEATRICE

Never gone forth? O, I can think no
    more!
It was too long, so long, too long ago!
I am near death; but you should tell me
    truth;
Is it that you forgive me, or deceive,
Unwilling I should know it?

THE ABBESS

              None deceives,
None pardons. We have seen you every
    day
Before the altar punctual, to our hours
Attentive, and to all the humble cares
Of alms and of the threshold.

Sister Beatrice

BEATRICE

I am here,

My Mother, and I do not think I dream.

Look at this hand : I tear it with my nails ;

See, the blood shows and flows ; the blood
is real.

I have no other proofs.   So tell me now,

If you have pity, here, in face of God,

For we are close to God when people die,—

If you do wish it, I will say no more,

But if you can for pity tell me, now,

What did you say, and what it was you
did

When five-and-twenty years ago you
found

One morning that the door was opened
wide,

The corridor deserted—when you found

The altar abandoned—when you found
the veil,

The veil and mantle ? . . . Mother, I can
no more.

88

Sister Beatrice

THE ABBESS

Daughter, this memory, I understand,
Must trouble you and overwhelm you
    still,
Though five-and-twenty years ago befell
The wondrous miracle whereby your God
Elected you.   The Virgin left us then,
To mount again to heaven; ere she went
Investing you with her most holy robe
And sacred ornaments, and lastly crowned
You with her golden crown, to teach us
    so
In boundless mercy that while she was
    gone
You took her place.

BEATRICE

          But who then took my place?

THE ABBESS

Why, no one took it, since you still were
    there.

Sister Beatrice

BEATRICE

There, every day?   I was among you all?
I moved, I spoke, you touched me with
　　your hands?

THE ABBESS

As now, my child, I touch you with my
　　hand.

BEATRICE

Mother, I know no more; except I think
I have no longer strength to understand.
I am still submissive, and I ask you naught.
I feel that all are very good : I feel
That death is very gentle.

　　　　　　　　　　Is it you
Who understand the soul is wretched—
　　you?
There was no pardon here when here I
　　lived.
I have said often, when I was not happy,
God would not punish if He once knew all.
But you are happy, and have learned it all.

Sister Beatrice

In other days all folk ignored distress,
In other days they cursed all those that
    sinned ;
But now all pardon, and all seem to
    know . . .
One of the angels, one would almost say,
Had spoken out the truth. Mother, and
    you,
My Sister Eglantine, give me your hands—
You are not angry with me?   Tell them all,
My sisters . . . what is it they should be
    told ?
My eyes no longer open, and my lips
Stiffen. . . . At last I fall asleep.   I have
    lived
In a world wherein I knew not what de-
    sired
Hate and ill-will, and in another world
I die, and understand not what desire,
Nor whereat aim mercy and love.

> [*She falls back exhausted among the
>   sheets.   Silence.*

Sister Beatrice

SISTER EGLANTINE
                                    She sleeps.

THE ABBESS

Pray, pray, my sisters, till the triumphant
   hour!
          [*The* NUNS *fall on their knees around
                the bed of* BEATRICE.

THE END OF SISTER BEATRICE